Junie B., First Grader
Aloha-ha-ha!

Check out Barbara Park's other funny books, listed at the end of this book!

BARBARA PARK

Junie B., First Grader®
Aloha-ha-ha!

illustrated by Denise Brunkus

A STEPPING STONE BOOK™

Random House New York

To *the totally indispensable, completely irreplaceable,*
occasionally excitable, but always lovable . . .
Cathy Goldsmith

Copyright © 2006 by Barbara Park
Illustrations copyright © 2006 by Denise Brunkus

Published in the United States by Random House Children's Books,
a division of Random House, Inc., New York.

RANDOM HOUSE and colophon are registered trademarks and A STEPPING
STONE BOOK and colophon are trademarks of Random House, Inc.
JUNIE B., FIRST GRADER stylized design is a registered trademark of Barbara
Park, used under license.

www.randomhouse.com/junieb
www.randomhouse.com/kids

Educators and librarians, for a variety of teaching tools, visit us at
www.randomhouse.com/teachers

Library of Congress Cataloging-in-Publication Data
Park, Barbara.
Junie B., first grader : Aloha-ha-ha! / by Barbara Park ; illustrated by
Denise Brunkus. — 1st ed.
    p.   cm. (Junie B. Jones series ; #26)
SUMMARY: Excitable Junie B. Jones manages to find trouble both before
and during a trip to Hawaii and records each incident in a photo journal
given to her by her teacher.
ISBN: 0-375-83403-6 (trade) — ISBN: 0-375-93403-0 (lib. bdg.)
ISBN-13: 978-0-375-83403-5 (trade) —
ISBN-13: 978-0-375-93403-2 (lib. bdg.)
[1. Vacations—Fiction. 2. Hawaii—Fiction. 3. Photojournalism—Fiction.
4. Schools—Fiction. 5. Diaries—Fiction.]   I. Title: Aloha-ha-ha.
II. Brunkus, Denise, ill. III. Title.
PZ7.P2197Jqs 2001   [Fic]—dc22   2005023707

Printed in the United States of America
10 9 8 7 6 5 4 3 2 1 First Edition

Contents

1

■ ■ ■ ■ ■ ■ ■ ■ ■ ■

Flinging

Friday

Dear first-grade journal,
  I'VE GOT BIG NEWS!
  I'VE GOT BIG NEWS!
  Last night Daddy told me a
happy surprise. And it's called
my family is going on an
exciting ~~vakashum~~ vacation! And it is
going to be the time of our life,
I tell you!

> *I am trying to save my news for Show and Tell. But I don't think I can wait that long. That is how come I am going to ask my teacher to start that activity RIGHT EXACTLY NOW!*
>
> *Please stand by . . .*

I stopped writing and raised my hand.

Mr. Scary was not looking at me.

When teachers don't look, you have to stand up and shout. Or else how are they supposed to notice you?

I stood up and shouted.

"MR. S.! MR. S.! HOW LONG UNTIL WE HAVE SHOW-AND-TELL, DO YOU THINK?"

Mr. Scary wrinkled his eyebrows at me.

I am not supposed to call him *Mr. S.*, I believe.

"Please sit down, Junie B.," he said. "It's still journal time. And journal time is quiet time."

I nodded. "Yeah, I know. Only I'd actually like to wrap things up and get started with Show-and-Tell now."

Mr. Scary sucked in his cheeks.

"Sit *down*," he said again. "We will have Show-and-Tell shortly."

I looked at the clock. "How many minutes is shortly?" I asked. "Is it one minute or eight minutes or eleven minutes? On account of if it's one minute, I can wait, probably. But eleven minutes would be out of the question."

Mr. Scary walked back to my desk. And he sat me in my chair.

I glanced up at him. "All I'm looking for is a rough estimate," I said.

Just then, my neighbor named May leaned across the aisle. And she did a giant SHH! in my face.

I quick wiped my cheek.

"EW!" I hollered. "EW! EW! EW!"

'Cause May got *spittle* on me, that's why! And *spittle* is the grown-up word for spitooey!

I zoomed to the back of the room. And I climbed on the stool to reach the faucet. But Mr. Scary beat me to it.

He wet a paper towel and wiped my face.

"Thank you," I said. "I needed that."

Mr. Scary rolled his eyes.

"You're being very rambunctious this morning, aren't you, Junie B. Jones?" he said.

I scratched my head at that vocabulary.

"Okay. You lost me on that one," I said.

"Rambunctious," he repeated. "*Rambunctious* means—"

May's voice interrupted.

"BAD!" she called out. "'*Bunctious* means *bad,* Junie Jones! You're being bad this morning! Bad, bad, bad, bad, bad!"

I turned to look at her.

Her chair was spun around to face the back of the room.

She was watching me like an audience.

Mr. Scary ran his fingers through his tired hair.

Then he went to May's desk. And he turned her back in the right direction.

Teachers spend a lot of time adjusting people.

After he came back, he bent down next to me. And he made his voice more private.

"Junie B., I know why you're excited," he whispered. "Your mother called me on the phone last night. And she told me about your vacation next week."

I threw out my arms real thrilled. And I flinged myself way high in the air.

"I can't *wait*, Mr. Scary! I can't wait! I can't wait!" I said.

Mr. Scary grabbed my arms. And he kept me from flinging.

"Okay. See, this is the wild behavior that I'm talking about," he said. "I *really* need you to stay calm until Show-and-Tell, Junie B. Can you do that for me, please?"

I thought for a second. Then I shrugged my shoulders.

"Yeah, only I don't actually *know* if I can do that," I said. "'Cause I'm already *trying* to be calm. And this is how I'm turning out."

My teacher tapped on his chin.

"Hmm. Maybe we could make a deal," he said. "How 'bout this? If you stay quiet and calm until Show-and-Tell, I'll let you go first. How does that sound?"

I bounced up and down at that exciting idea.

"That sounds like a D-E-E-L!" I said.

"You mean D-E-A-L," said Mr. Scary. "*Deal* is spelled with an *a*, Junie B."

"Whatever," I said.

After that, I twirled real fast in a happy circle. And I accidentally spun myself into the ground.

On my way down, I knocked over the trash can and the sink stool.

All of Room One turned to look at me.

I sat up and waved my fingers.

"Do not be alarmed, people. I am perfectly okay," I said.

After that, I stood up and dusted myself off. Then I went back to my seat.

I looked at the clock again.

No minutes had passed at all, hardly.

I put my head down and did a groan.

Time is as slow as a turtle.

2

Pair-o-Dice

The children wrote in their journals forever, it seemed.

Then finally, finally, *finally* . . . they started to finish!

And at last!

IT WAS TIME FOR SHOW-AND-TELL!

My legs sprang up. And they ran me to the front of the room.

Then I flinged myself in the air again. And I shouted, "VACATION! VACATION! I'M GOING ON A VACATION!"

Only too bad for me. 'Cause when I came down from my fling, I lost my balance. And I landed on the floor again.

This time, Room One laughed their heads off.

I tapped my fingers real annoyed.

"Okay . . . I've really got to knock off the flinging," I said to just myself.

Mr. Scary quieted everyone down.

"Boys and girls, the reason Junie B. is so excited today is that she didn't find out about her vacation until just *last night*."

He winked at me. "Tell everyone where you're going, Junie B."

I took a big breath.

Then the words came hollering out!

"HAWAII, PEOPLE! I'M GOING TO HAWAII! AND I AM GOING THIS VERY *EXACT SUNDAY*!"

All of the children's mouths fell open.

Except for, not richie Lucille's.

Instead, Lucille stretched her arms in the air. And she did a giant yawn.

"Hawaii. Ho-hum. Been there . . . done that," she said real bored.

Then she stood up.

And she twirled around.

And she sat back down again.

My friend named Shirley stood up, too.

"Well, *I've* never been there!" she said. "I can't believe it, Junie B.! You're really, really going to Hawaii?"

"Yes, Shirley! Really!" I said. "This was the biggest surprise of my career, I tell you! On account of last night Daddy said he is going on a job interview in Hawaii! And he surprised me and Mother with two extra tickets!"

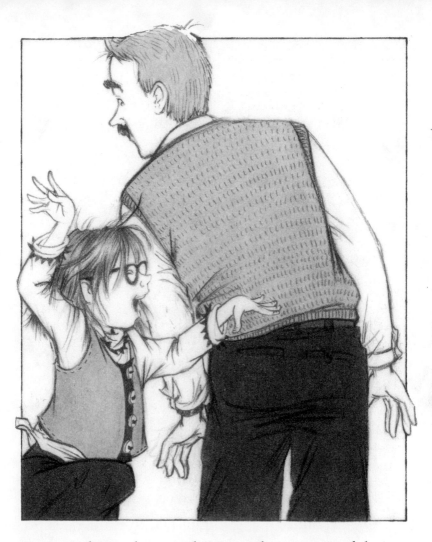

I skipped around my teacher very joyful.
"And that is not even the bestest part
yet!" I said. "Because Daddy told me that

this trip is for 'big people' only! And so my baby brother named Ollie is not even *allowed*!"

Room One looked shocked at that information.

"Wow!" said my friend José. "You mean you're *big people,* Junie B.?"

I nodded my head real fast.

"Oh yes, José. I am *big people,* all right," I said. "That's how come I got to read the travel booklet with Mother last night. And the travel booklet says Hawaii is a real, actual *paradise.*"

Mr. Scary grinned.

"A *paradise,* huh? That's a great word, Junie B. Does everyone know what a paradise is?"

Sheldon shot his hand in the air.

"I do! I do!" he shouted. "My grampa

Ned Potts has a pair-o-dice! He used to play craps at the gambling casino. But then someone squealed to Gramma. And so now he's not allowed out at night anymore."

May jumped up and pointed.

"Sheldon said a bad word! Sheldon said a bad word!" she tattled real loud.

Mr. Scary stared at her.

"May, dear . . . I'm very sorry to ruin this special tattling moment for you," he said. "But Sheldon did *not* say a bad word. *Craps* is a dice game that's played at gambling casinos."

May stood there a second. "Well, at least I gave it a shot," she said. Then she did a shrug and sat back down.

After that, Mr. Scary printed the word PARADISE on the board.

He turned and looked at Sheldon.

"And, Sheldon, my friend," he said, "the word is *paradise*. Not *pair-o-dice*."

Sheldon did a shrug, too.

"I don't think Gramma really cares how you spell it," he said. "Grampa's still not getting out at night."

Mr. Scary closed his eyes a minute.

Then he went to the sink. And he got a drink of water.

On his way back, he stopped at the world map on our bulletin board. And he showed Room One where Hawaii is.

"Boys and girls, these Pacific islands are the main islands that make up the state of Hawaii," he told us.

He got the world globe off the shelf. And he asked me to carry it around to show the children.

I stopped at each desk.

"Whoa!" said Roger. "Hawaii looks like a bunch of little dots floating in the ocean."

I nodded. "I know it, Roger," I said. "But my mother said the dots are bigger in person."

Mr. Scary laughed. "Oh, they're *much* bigger in person, Junie B. And they're not really *floating*, Roger. So don't worry. Our friend Junie B. won't be drifting away."

May did a grump noise. "Phooey," she said.

I ignored that situation. Instead, I put the globe back. And I went to the front of the room again.

"I know other information about Hawaii, too," I said. "Mother read that there are lots of flowers and birds there. Plus also, she read that Hawaii was formed by exploding volcanoes."

I thought for a second. "She read a bunch of other junk, too. But I finally got bored and tuned her out."

Mr. Scary did a chuckle.

"Well, volcanoes are pretty interesting, really. When volcanoes erupt, they spew out lava. And over millions of years, lava can form landmasses," he explained. "As a matter of fact, there are still two active volcanoes in Hawaii right now."

I stood there real quiet. And I let that information sink in my head.

Then, all of a sudden, I did a little shiver.

"Okay, see, I wasn't actually aware of an eruption problem," I said.

May jumped up again.

"Well, I'm sure glad that *I'm* not going to Hawaii," she hollered. "Who wants to get erupted on by a spewy, hot volcano? Getting erupted on by a spewy, hot volcano would ruin your whole vacation trip."

Mr. Scary sucked in his cheeks.

"Junie B. is *not* going to get erupted on by a 'spewy, hot volcano,' May," he said. "There are no active volcanoes on the island where Junie B. is going."

May thought a minute.

"Okay, fine. But let's just say that she *did* get erupted on by a spewy, hot volcano. That would definitely ruin her whole vacation trip. True or false?"

Mr. Scary went to the sink again.

This time, he splashed water on his face.

After he dried off, he put May back in her chair.

I waved my hand to talk some more.

"Yeah, only I didn't even tell everyone the most exciting part yet! 'Cause guess how I'm getting to Hawaii, people? Guess, guess, guess!" I said. "No, wait! I will give you a hint!"

After that, I straightened out my arms like wings. And I zoomed around Room One.

"See me, people? See me? I'm flying! I'm flying! *That's* how I'm getting to Hawaii! I'm flying in a real, actual *airplane*!"

Lucille stood up and did another yawn.

"Airplane, shmairplane," she said. "Tell me something I *haven't* done."

Mr. Scary sat her down.

"This is going to be an amazing adventure for you, Junie B.," he told me.

He grinned real big.

"And—just to be sure that you bring back lots of wonderful pictures—I bought you a little gift for your trip."

He went to the closet and took out a
shopping bag.

I hurried and peeked inside.

And wowie wow wow!

There was a camera in that thing!

I quick pulled it out and showed the
class.

"Look, people! Look! It's the kind of

camera that you get at the drugstore!" I said. "I am *excellent* at this equipment! 'Cause I already used one on my class field trip in kindergarten!"

After that, Mr. Scary reached into the bag and pulled out another gift.

"And take a look at *this*, Junie B. This is called a *photo journal*," he said. "A photo journal is similar to the first-grade journals we use in class each day. Except a photo journal tells a story in *photographs* instead of words."

He opened it up for me. "See inside? Each page has a place for a daily picture and a caption. A *caption* is another name for a picture title," he explained.

He showed the album to the class.

"Every day, Junie B. will take a picture of what she did on her trip," he said. "Then she will organize her photos and give them captions. And when she comes back to school, her photo journal will tell us the story of her exciting trip to paradise!"

He handed me my album.

"Doesn't that sound like a fun assignment, Junie B.?" he asked.

I started to nod.

Then suddenly, I stopped.

'Cause something did not sound right about that sentence.

I tapped on my chin.

It was the word *assignment*, I believe.

Finally, I looked at my teacher.

"Okay, here is the problem," I said. "*Assignment* means schoolwork, and *Hawaii* means vacation. And children do not actually like to mix those two items."

Mr. Scary smiled. "Oh, but this will be a

fun assignment, Junie B.," he said. "And it's a very *special* assignment, too. You're going to be Room One's first *official* photo journalist."

My ears perked up.

"Official?" I said. "Did you say the word *official*?"

He grinned. "Yes. I did. That's exactly what I said . . . *official*."

I looked at him again. "*Official* means *important*, right?"

"Oh yes," he said. "You can't get much more important than being *official*."

I stood up a little bit straighter.

Official makes you automatically taller, I think.

After that, Mr. Scary shook my hand. And he walked me back to my seat.

"Oh," he said. "And don't forget to take

your first-grade journal to Hawaii with you, okay, Junie B.? It would be a terrible shame to miss a whole week of journal writing, wouldn't it?"

I looked at him real strange.

Teachers and children do not have the same kind of brains.

Finally, I did a sigh. And I took out my journal. And I dropped it in the bag with my camera.

My friend named Herbert turned around very excited.

"You're a lucky duck, Junie B. Jones!" he said. "I wish *I* was going to Hawaii next week!"

"Me too!" said Lennie.

"Me three!" said José.

I looked at May.

She did not say, "Me four."

Instead, she just kept staring straight ahead. And she didn't talk at all.

I did a shrug and went back to my own business.

Then suddenly—without any warning—May shot her arms into the air. And she hollered the word "KABOOM!"

She looked at me and smiled.

"That was the sound of a spewy, hot volcano erupting on you," she said.

I sat there a second.

Then I did another shiver.

May is not amusing.

3

New Friend

The next day was Saturday.

I woke up with ants in my pants.

'Cause just one more day till Hawaii, of course!

After breakfast, me and Mother packed my suitcase for the trip. Also, we stuffed crayons and toys in my backpack for the airplane.

"This plane ride is going to be fun! Right, Mother? Right?" I said. "This plane ride is going to be the time of my life!"

Mother sighed.

"Well, it's *definitely* going to be long. That's for sure," she said. "And it could get a little boring, too, I'm afraid."

She stood there a minute. Then she winked at me.

"*That's* why I got you a brand-new friend for the trip, Junie B.," she said.

My eyes lighted up very thrilled.

"A new friend?" I said. "You got me a new friend?"

She ruffled my hair.

"I sure did. Wait here and I'll go get her," she said.

As soon as she left, I grabbed my favorite stuffed elephant named Philip Johnny Bob. And I danced him all around the room.

"A new friend, Philip! I'm getting a new friend!" I sang real happy.

Philip sucked in his cheeks.

You don't need a new friend, Junie B. You have me, remember? I am your friend.

I hugged him very tight.

"Yes, I *know* you are my friend, Phil," I said. "But it's still nice to make other friends, too. Right?"

Wrong, said Philip. *You only need me. And that's all.*

Just then, Mother came back with my new friend.

And my whole mouth came open, I tell you!

"A HULA GIRL BARBIE! IT'S A HULA GIRL BARBIE! I'VE ALWAYS, ALWAYS WANTED ONE OF THESE THINGS!" I said. "THANK YOU, MOTHER! THANK YOU! THANK YOU! THANK YOU!"

I looked at Barbie through her box.

"Wow! Look! She has her very own hula

skirt! And her very own hula sandals! Plus also, she's got a hula wreath around her neck!"

Mother smiled.

"It's not a *hula wreath,* Junie B. It's called a *lei,*" she said. "A lei is a necklace made of flowers. We'll see lots of them in Hawaii."

I took Hula Girl Barbie out of her box. And I danced around some more.

"I think I will name her Delores," I said. "*Delores* has a nice ring to it."

Finally, I stopped dancing. And I introduced her to Philip.

"Philip Johnny Bob, meet Hula Girl Delores," I said.

Hello, said Delores.

Whatever, said Philip.

After that, I put both of those guys in my

backpack. And I zipped them up real tight.

"Now I won't even be boring on the plane! Right, Mother? Right? 'Cause first I will color. And then I will play with Hula Girl Delores. Plus also, I can take some pictures of the plane with my photo-journal camera!"

Mother gave me a hug. And she went to her room to pack her own suitcase.

As soon as she was gone, a scuffle broke out in my backpack.

I opened it up to see the trouble.

Philip said to please get him out of there *right exactly now*. On account of Hula Girl Delores was poking him with her pointy, hard hands.

I took him out and put him on my bed.

"Okay. You can stay out here for one more day, Phil," I said. "But tomorrow you're going to *have* to ride in the backpack with Delores. Or else you won't be able to fly to Hawaii with us."

Just then, chill bumps came on my arms.

"Hawaii, Phil," I whispered. "We're really, really, really going to Hawaii."

After that, I jumped off my bed.

And I straightened out my arms.

And I zoomed around my room like I was flying some more.

The next morning, we took baby Ollie to my grandma and grampa Miller's house. 'Cause that is where *his* vacation was going to be.

I kissed him goodbye. And I pretended I would miss him.

"Goodbye, little Ollie. I wish you could come with us," I said real sad.

Everyone smiled at me.

Nice fibs are okay to say, I think. Only I'm not sure of the exact ruling on that.

After all of us said goodbye, me and Mother and Daddy drove to the airport.

And then what do you know?

We started waiting in a million jillion lines.

First, we waited in the "getting our car into the parking lot" line. Then we waited in the shuttle-bus line, and the "give the man your suitcase" line, and the "get your boarding passes here" line.

After that, there was just one more line to go. It is called the "now we're going to look through all of your stuff with our X-ray vision" line.

That line is exactly like the lines at Disneyland, except for it's longer. Plus there's no actual ride at the end.

While I waited, I unzipped my backpack. And I checked on my toys.

Philip Johnny Bob made grumpy elephant eyes at me.

Delores keeps poking me. Tell her to stop poking me, he grouched.

He turned back to Delores. And he did a *grr*.

Stay on your own side of the backpack, and I mean it, he said.

Just then, Daddy grabbed my backpack.

He quick zipped it up. And he shoved it into the X-ray-vision machine.

Only too bad for Philip Johnny Bob. 'Cause he wasn't actually expecting that situation. And the machine was very dark inside.

HEY! WHO TURNED OUT THE LIGHTS? he shouted. *GET ME OUT OF*

HERE! GET ME OUT OF HERE!

Suddenly, the X-ray-vision man stopped the machine.

"Who said that?" he snapped. "Is someone trying to play games?"

Daddy did a little smile.

"Oh, uh . . . actually my daughter here said it," he told him. "Sometimes she pretends that she's, well . . . you know . . . *a stuffed elephant.*"

The X-ray-vision man looked at Daddy real suspicious.

Then a lady pulled us out of the line.

And she made us hold out our arms.

And she waved a giant wand all around ourselves.

I clapped very thrilled.

"Hey! This is just like *America's Most Wanted*!" I said.

The lady said *this was not a joke, little miss.*

I stopped clapping.

The airport does not have a good sense of humor.

4

■ ■ ■ ■ ■ ■ ■ ■ ■ ■

Being a Sandwich

After we got to our plane gate, we waited and waited some more.

Then at last! A man said it was time for us to board the airplane!

Board the airplane is the airport word for *What do you know? Another dumb-bunny line!*

Only good news!

This time, we were near the front! And so finally, finally, *finally* . . . we got to our seats!

"I GET THE WINDOW SEAT! I GET

THE WINDOW SEAT!" I called real loud.

Then I ran there speedy quick. And I sat right down.

There was a teensy little shade on the window!

I pushed it up and pulled it down.

It was a little bit stuckish.

That's how come I kept pushing and pulling and pushing and pulling until it loosened up.

Pretty soon, I tapped on Mother and Daddy.

"Watch me, okay? Watch me work the window shade!" I said.

I took a big breath and started right in.

"Up and down! Up and down! Up and down!" I said.

I stopped and breathed again.

Then I speeded up a little bit.

"Upanddown upanddown, upanddown upanddown upand—"

Just then, Mother reached out her hand. And she stopped my progress.

"Okay, good . . . fine. Excellent shade work. Thank you very much," she said.

Then she buckled my seat belt.

I stretched out my legs as long as they would go.

And guess what?

They reached all the way to the seat in front of me!

"Whoa! My legs are as tall as a giant!" I said.

I flattened my feet against the seat. And I pushed and stretched some more.

Then, all of a sudden, the lady in front of me popped up like a jumping jack! And she spun around real angry.

"Would you *please* stop kicking my seat?" she grouched. "I don't like having my seat kicked."

Mother quick took my legs down.

"Oh my. Sorry," she said. "It's her first plane trip."

I looked at Mother very curious.

"But I wasn't even *kicking* her seat," I said. "My legs were just being tall."

The lady made a *harrumph* sound. And she turned around again.

After that, I stayed real still. And I didn't move my muscles.

Only wait a second! Hold the phone!

Just then, I spotted the cutest thing I ever saw!

And it's called, *Hey! There's a little tray on the back of the grouchy lady's seat! And it's folded up real flat!*

I leaned up and opened it. "Ha! What will they think of next?" I said.

I practiced folding it in and out.

"Watch me, Mother! Watch me, Daddy!" I said.

I stood up tall to demonstrate.

"In and out . . . in and out . . . in and out . . . in and—"

BAM!

The grouchy lady popped up again.

"What in heaven's name are you doing *now?*" she grouched.

I did a gulp.

"I'm demonstrating my tray table," I said.

Mother's face looked embarrassed.

She said she is sorry again.

The lady did a snort and turned back around.

"*Please,* Junie B.," said Mother. "Behave yourself. Do not touch that lady's seat one more time."

I slumped way down in my seat.

Then I reached into my backpack. And I pulled out Philip Johnny Bob. And I whispered in his softie ear.

"Do not touch that seat right there. Or a grouchy lady will snap your trunk off," I said.

41

Philip raised his eyebrows.

I can't touch it? he asked. *Not even with my little pinkie toe?*

I thought for a second.

"Well, okay. I guess you can touch it with your little pinkie toe. But that's all," I said.

And so very careful, Philip reached out.

And he touched the lady's seat with his pinkie toe.

And ha!

She didn't feel a thing!

Me and Philip laughed and laughed at that funny joke.

Then pretty soon, he tapped on his chin. And he looked curious at me again.

Hmm. I wonder if there's a grouchy lady behind us, too? he asked.

I shrugged my shoulders. "I don't know,

Phil. Why don't you take a peek?" I said.

And so Philip Johnny Bob turned around. And he tried to peek through the seat crack. But he couldn't get a good look.

So finally, I had to lift him way up to the top of my seat. And I let him stare back there for a while.

Only, bad news. It didn't actually work out that good. On account of we forgot that Phil's eyes are buttons. And buttons do not have good distance vision.

He came back very glum. *Phooey,* he said. *I couldn't see a thing. Now what?*

I thought some more.

Then yay! A little light bulb went on in my head! And I quick reached my hand into my backpack again. And I took out Hula Girl Delores!

"Phil! Phil! It's Delores! It's Delores!"

I said. "Delores is skinny enough to fit through the seat space! See? Plus her eyes are not even buttons!"

Philip smiled. *You are sharp as a tack, Junie B.,* he said.

"I know it, Philip! I know I am sharp as a tack. And so I will send Delores on a spy mission to the seat behind us," I said. "Please stand by."

After that, I picked up Delores. And I pushed her through the seat space. And I let her take a nice long peek.

Only just then, a little bit of trouble happened.

And it's called, *I felt a tug on Delores's head.*

And then whoosh!

Someone pulled her to the other side of the seat!

I could not believe my eyeballs at that situation!

Very quick, I got on my knees. And me and Philip looked over the top of my seat.

And oh no, oh no!

Another grouchy lady was staring back at us!

She was holding Delores in her hand. And her face was not smiling.

She did a frown at me.

"You're a little bit old to be playing peekaboo, don't you think?" she grumped.

I did another gulp.

"Yeah, only we weren't even playing peekaboo," I said.

We were on a spy mission, said Philip Johnny Bob.

Just then, Daddy stood up. And said a 'pology to the woman. And he got Delores back for me.

Then he sat me back in my seat. And he said if I do not behave myself, we will turn this plane right around. And we won't even *go* to Hawaii!

I looked and looked at that man.

That was a bluff, I think.

After that, I put Delores away in my backpack. And me and Philip whispered to each other real secret.

"I can't believe it, Phil," I said. "There's a grouchy lady in front of us and a grouchy lady behind us."

Philip did a sigh. *We're right in the middle of a grouchy lady sandwich.*

We slumped down in our seat. And we looked out the window.

Then whew! At last! The pilot talked over the loudspeakers. And he said we are next in line for takeoff!

Me and Philip hugged each other real happy.

And then, yippee! The engines got very loud.

And the plane started to move.

And we went faster and faster and faster!

And . . . HA!

WE WENT ALL THE WAY UP IN THE SKY!

It was just like a magic carpet, I tell you! There were puffy clouds wherever I looked!

"THIS VIEW TAKES MY BREATHING AWAY!" I hollered to Mother and Daddy.

Mother smiled. "Yes, it does," she said. "But you don't have to shout."

I pointed at my ears.

"YEAH, ONLY THERE'S AIRPLANE NOISE IN MY HEAD! AND SO I CAN'T ACTUALLY HEAR MY OWN VOICE!" I explained.

Mother picked up my backpack.

"Well, let's try to find something quiet to do, okay?"

"OKAY!" I said back.

We looked through all the stuff I brought.

Then hurray, hurray!

I spotted my brand-new camera!

"WOW! I ALMOST FORGOT ABOUT THAT ASSIGNMENT!" I said. "TODAY WILL BE THE FIRST OFFICIAL PICTURE FOR MY PHOTO JOURNAL!"

My eyes lighted up.

"HEY! I KNOW! YOU CAN TAKE A PICTURE OF ME BY THE WINDOW! OKAY, MOTHER? OKAY? A PICTURE OF ME BY THE WINDOW WILL BE THE PERFECT START!"

Mother put her finger to her lips.

"Shh! You're still talking too loudly, Junie B. Everyone can hear you," she said.

After that, she took out the camera. And she started to aim.

"NO! NO! WAIT! HOLD IT! I DIDN'T EVEN GET POSED YET!" I told her.

I quick undid my seat belt and leaned next to the window.

"GET THE CLOUDS IN THE BACK-GROUND, OKAY, MOTHER? ROOM ONE WILL LOVE TO SEE ME WAY UP HIGH IN THE CLOUDS!"

Philip Johnny Bob was still sitting on the seat.

I reached over and picked him up.

"AND GET PHILIP, TOO! OKAY? JUST ME . . . AND PHILIP . . . AND THE CLOUDS . . . AND THAT'S ALL," I said.

Just then, Philip tapped on me. And he whispered a funny secret.

I started to laugh.

Then I told the funny secret to Mother.

"PLUS PHILIP SAYS DON'T GET THE GROUCHY LADIES!" I said. "'CAUSE THOSE TWO GROUCHPOTS WILL RUIN MY WHOLE ENTIRE PHOTO JOURNAL."

Mother's eyes got big and wide at me.

"SHH! JUNIE B.! *PLEASE!*" she said, very panicked.

Then she quick tried to take the picture.

But oh no!

Both of those grouches sprang up as fast as springs!

AND THEIR BIG GRUMPHEADS GOT RIGHT IN MY PICTURE!

I covered my mouth real shocked.

Mother covered her mouth real shocked, too.

Then both of us kept our heads bent down, until the grouches stopped staring.

51

After they were gone, I looked at Mother.

"Me and my big fat mouth," I said in a whisper.

Mother kept her head down, and she talked to me through her fingers.

"I couldn't have put it better myself," she said.

After that, she gave me back my camera. And she said that maybe we would try again later . . . *after the dust settled.*

I did a sigh.

"Yeah, only I *can't* try again later," I said real whiny. "On account of I need to save the rest of the pictures for Hawaii."

I slumped down very glum.

Then I closed my eyes.

And I thought about that stupid dumb picture caption.

Day One: GROUCHY LADIES.

I did a cringe.

My photo journal was *not* off to a good start.

5

■ ■ ■ ■ ■ ■ ■ ■ ■

Tight Fit

The plane ride took forever and ever.

Me and Philip Johnny Bob ran out of stuff to play with.

Then finally, we took a teensy little nap.

And when we woke up . . .

At last!

We were at Hawaii!

And wait till you hear *this*!

As soon as we got off the plane, some Hawaii people gave us flower leis! And that is just plain friendly, I tell you!

After Mother and Daddy got our suitcases, we rented a car. And we drove to a pretty hotel.

A man in a uniform opened the door for us.

"Aloha," he said real nice.

"Alo-*who?*" I said back.

"Alo*ha*," said the man. "*Aloha* is the Hawaiian word for hello and goodbye."

I smiled. "Hey! I like that word of *aloha*," I said. "It sounds like it's laughing, sort of. Alo*ha*! Ha-ha!"

After that, I skipped inside the hotel. And my eyes popped right out of my head.

'Cause wowie wow wow! It was the most beautiful 'stablishment I ever even saw!

It had lots of colorful flowers! And tall, skinny palm trees! Plus outside, there were two different kinds of water!

First, there was an ocean with a real, actual beach. Plus also, there was a swimming pool with a real, actual diving board!

And that is not even the end of the beauty!

On account of—when we went to our room—there were two giant beds the size of a queen!

I threw out my arms real joyful.

"Hawaii!" I said. "You gotta love it!"

Then I twirled and twirled. And I crashed into one of the beds. And I fell on the softie carpet.

It was very thick and plushy.

I did a yawn.

Then I curled up very comfortable.

And I closed my eyes.

Daddy came over and picked me up.

Then Mother put me to bed.

And I slept all the way till morning.

The sun shined in my eyes.

I stretched very sleepy. And I looked all around the beautiful room.

Then bingo!

I remembered!

"I AM IN HAWAII!" I said.

I jumped out of bed. And I jiggled Mother and Daddy awake.

"ALOHA-HA-HA, PEOPLE! ALOHA-HA-HA!" I hollered. "WE'RE IN HAWAII! WE'RE IN HAWAII!"

After that, I ran to the window. And I looked at all the water.

"Let's go to the pool! Let's go to the pool!" I hollered again.

Mother and Daddy sat up and yawned. Then they looked at each other. And they flopped back on their pillows again.

Old people on vacation are not that fun.

I did a big breath at those two.

Then I went to their bed. And I jiggled them some more till they got up. Then *finally*, they got dressed. And we went to a restaurant for breakfast.

And YIPPEE! YIPPEE! HOORAY!

RIGHT AFTER WE ATE, IT WAS TIME FOR THE POOL!

Only here is the happiest part of all!

On our way to the pool, we passed a gift-shop window. And I saw the cutest swim ring in the whole entire world!

"Mother! Daddy! Look at that swim ring! It looks exactly like a parrot! See it? See it? Isn't it cute? Huh? Isn't it?"

The gift-shop lady heard me being gushy.

She took the swim ring out of the window. And she handed it to me.

"It's the last one we have," she said.

I jumped up and down very urgent.

"The last one! The last one! Can I have it, Mother? Can I have it, Daddy? Please? Please? Please?" I said. "If you buy me this swim ring, I won't ask for one other thing! Not for this whole entire trip!"

Mother and Daddy looked suspicious at me.

'Cause that was a fib, of course.

"But you don't even *need* a swim ring, Junie B.," said Daddy. "You learned how to swim two years ago."

"Exactly," said Mother. "Plus this swim ring is way too small for you, honey. It's meant for children much younger than you are."

I jumped up and down some more.

"But I *know* I can fit in this thing, Mother. I just know I can! I am thin as a noodle!"

I folded my hands real begging.

"Please, can I have it? Please, please, please?"

Daddy ran his fingers through his hair.

That is a good sign, usually.

Then finally, he took my parrot swim ring. And he gave the gift lady some money.

I hugged and hugged him very happy.

"Thank you, Daddy! Thank you! Thank you! You are the nicest daddy in the whole entire world!"

After that, I skipped to the pool with my parrot swim ring. And I tried to put it on. But it was way too tight to fit.

Daddy watched what I was doing.

"It looks like your mother was right, Junie B.," he said. "That swim ring is much too small."

"No, it isn't, Daddy. I *know* I can fit into this parrot," I said. "I am positive I can."

I thought for a second.

Then I walked to the edge of the pool. And I dropped my swim ring in the water.

And *KERSPLASH!*

I jumped through the middle!
And what do you know?
I squeezed right in!
I clapped and clapped real thrilled.

"SEE, MOTHER? SEE, DADDY?" I called. "I TOLD YOU I COULD FIT IN THIS THING! I TOLD YOU!"

I took a breath.

"IT'S JUST A LITTLE BIT TIGHTISH AROUND MY MIDDLE. BUT I THINK I

CAN STILL BREATHE . . . POSSIBLY."

I pushed away from the edge. And I kicked to the other side.

"DID YOU SEE ME SWIM OVER HERE, MOTHER? ARE YOU WATCHING ME, DADDY? THIS PARROT IS SPEEDY FAST!"

My stomach did a wince.

"ALSO, I AM IN SEVERE PAIN!" I shouted.

After that, I hurried up out of the pool. And I rushed to Mother speedy quick.

"Please get this off of me, right exactly *now*! 'Cause this thing is squeezing my insides in half!" I said.

And so she and Daddy tried to wiggle it off of me. But the parrot didn't budge itself.

I sucked in my tummy as skinny as it would go.

Then all of us pushed and pulled. And yanked and tugged. And twisted and stretched. Plus also, I jumped up and down.

After that, I panicked and shouted.

"I'M STUCK IN MY PARROT! I'M STUCK IN MY PARROT! 911! I'M STUCK IN MY PARROT!"

Everyone turned around to look.

"Shh!" said Daddy. "Stop shouting!"

Then he quick found the air plug.

And he opened it up.

And WHOOSH!

My parrot's air came rushing out!

Soon my stomach could breathe again.

"AHHH . . . *better*," I said. "Thank you, Daddy. Thank you."

I waited till all the air was out. Then I headed back to the pool.

Mother snapped her fingers at me.

"Whoa, wait a minute. You can't go in the pool like that, Junie B. We still need to get that swim ring off of you," she said. "You stay here. And I'll go get my scissors."

I raised up my eyebrows at that word.

"Scissors?" I said.

"Yes," said Mother. "I can cut that swim ring off of you in no time."

I let that information sink in.

Then, all of a sudden, my eyes got big and wide.

"NO, MOTHER! NO!" I shouted. "DON'T CUT MY PARROT OFF! PLEASE, PLEASE, PLEASE! IT DOESN'T EVEN HURT ANYMORE! I PROMISE! I PROMISE!"

Next to us, a grandpa did a frown. Plus his wife did a frown, too.

"For heaven's sake. What kind of mother

would cut a little girl's parrot?" said the grandpa.

"I don't know, Ed," said the grandma. "But it sure don't seem right."

Mother stood there kind of frozen.

Then she and Daddy picked up our pool towels. And we moved to different lounge chairs.

After that, Mother sat back down again. And she said she wouldn't get the scissors.

"Yay!" I said. "Yay! Yay!"

Then I jumped in the water. And I started to paddle.

"Look, Mother! Look! I'm still wearing my parrot! And it's not even squeezing my stomach!" I shouted. "Flatso parrots are perfectly comfortable."

I swam underwater to the end of the pool.

"THIS PARROT IS WORKING OUT BEAUTIFULLY!" I called again.

The grandma started to clap.

"Good for you! You showed her, didn't you?" she yelled.

Mother sat there a minute. Then she got up and moved our towels again.

I named my parrot Squeezer.

Squeezer was a flatso. But he was still fun to play with.

We swam and swam the whole entire day.

When it was time to leave, I gave my camera to Mother. And I asked her to take our picture for my photo-journal album.

"This will be a picture of my first new friend in Hawaii," I said.

I held up Squeezer's flatso head. And both of us said *cheese*.

Only too bad for me. Because just then, two boys walked by. And they pointed and laughed at flatso Squeezer.

"Duh, you're supposed to blow it up, doofus girl," said one of them.

The smile went off my face.

Mother snapped the picture.

Click-click.

Day Two: DOOFUS GIRL AND SQUEEZER.

6

Chicken of the Ocean

Day Three

Dear first-grade journal,

My camera pictures aren't going that good.

On account of first I got grouchy ladies. And then I looked like a doofus.

So far, my ~~foto~~ photo journal is telling the stupidest dumb story I ever heard of.

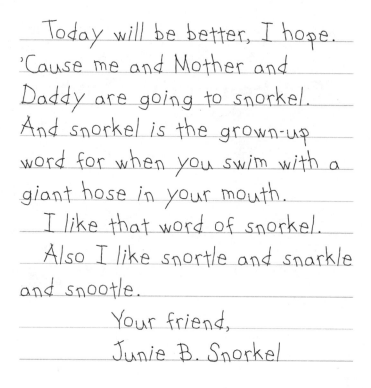

Today will be better, I hope.
'Cause me and Mother and
Daddy are going to snorkel.
And snorkel is the grown-up
word for when you swim with a
giant hose in your mouth.
   I like that word of snorkel.
   Also I like snortle and snarkle
and snootle.
            Your friend,
            Junie B. Snorkel

I put down my pencil. And I waited for
Mother and Daddy to get up.

Those two have lazy bones. Only I am
not allowed to jiggle them awake anymore.
Or else Mother turns out cranky.

I kept waiting real patient for their eyes to open.

Then finally, I tippytoed next to Daddy. And I blew air in his face.

He opened one eyeball.

I waved very pleasant.

"Hello. How are you today?" I said. "Look. I am already dressed for breakfast."

Daddy closed his eyeball.

I opened it up again.

"Whoops. I lost you there for a second," I said. "Don't you want to see what I'm wearing today?"

I stepped back so he could see my clothes. Then I twirled all around like a fashion girl.

"See me, Daddy? See how cute I look? I picked out an outfit to go with Squeezer's flatso parrot head. He looks very cute with these shorts, don't you think? He looks like a parrot belt . . . kind of."

I skipped around in a circle.

"I'm glad that Mother didn't cut him off," I said. "He wasn't even uncomfortable to sleep in, hardly."

After that, me and Squeezer climbed on the bed. And we sat on Mother's legs until she woke up.

It did not actually take that long.

Then yippee, hurray! All of us went down to breakfast. And Mother said I could order pineapple-and-coconut pancakes! And that is just like eating dessert, I tell you!

The waitress looked at me and Squeezer.

She did a little chuckle.

"Wow, you already have your swim ring on, huh?" she said. "All you have to do is blow him up, and you're all set to go."

I did a frown at that comment.

"Yeah, only I can't actually blow him up, or else he squeezes the life out of me," I said.

The waitress stopped smiling.

"Oh," she said. "Oh my."

Then she took our order. And she backed away from the table real slow.

After breakfast, Daddy had to go on his job interview. And so me and Mother went to the pool while we waited for him.

Then—as soon as he got back—hurray! It was time to go snorkeling!

After everyone was ready, we got in the car. And we drove to a special snorkel beach.

That word made me laugh in the car. I said it a million times, I think.

"Snorkel," I said. "Snorkel, snorkel,

snorkel. I'm going to snorkel! Here is a snorkel poem."

I took a breath.

"Snorkel, snortle, snootle, noodle, snorkel, snartle, snarkle."

Mother turned around.

"Please stop it," she said.

She took an aspirin.

Mothers do not appreciate poetry, apparently.

Pretty soon, Daddy pulled into a beach parking lot. And he carried our snorkel stuff to the water.

Mother helped me on with my swim fins.

Swim fins look exactly like frog feet. Except for they are not on an actual frog.

It is hard to walk in frog feet. You have to lift your feet way high in the air, like you are marching in a band. Except for frogs don't march in a band, usually. On account of most of them don't play an instrument.

After I put on my frog feet, I put on my face mask and snorkel snout.

A snorkel snout is the giant hose that you breathe with.

Then Daddy took me into the water. And we tightened my face mask.

And *ta-daa!*

I was ready to go!

I floated on top of the water. And I breathed through my snorkel snout.

I did very good with my breathing. 'Cause I already practiced this activity in the pool, that's why!

Only wowie wow wow!

I could *not* believe the view!

I raised up real excited.

"THE OCEAN BOTTOM IS WAY

PRETTIER THAN THE POOL BOT-
TOM!" I hollered. "YOU CAN SEE
CLEAR AS A BELT DOWN THERE!"

Mother and Daddy smiled. Then Daddy
said to please use my soft voice.

"Snorkeling is a *quiet* sport, Junie B.," he
said. "We don't want to bother the other
snorkelers, okay? So the word of the day is
quiet. Got it?"

"GOT IT!" I said. "THE WORD IS
QUIET!"

After that, I put on a snorkel vest to help
me float. And I held on to a kickboard. And
I swam with Mother and Daddy to a special
snorkel spot.

Frog feet help you swim speedy fast.

Even if you're swimming in a flatso
parrot, you can still be speedy.

After we got there, I put my head in the

water again. And my eyes popped out of my head!

The fish were *beeeauuutiful,* I tell you!

There were yellow ones! And blue ones! And orange ones! And silver ones! And black ones! And white ones! And spotted ones! And striped ones!

My heart pounded at the sight of them.

I raised my head and pulled out my snorkel snout.

"HEY! THIS IS JUST LIKE SWIM-MING IN THE FISH TANK AT MY SCHOOL!" I said.

Daddy quick put his finger to his lips. And he pointed to the other snorkelers.

"Shh! The word of the day is *quiet,* remember?" he said.

I tried to calm my voice. Only it kept on staying loud.

"YEAH, ONLY I DIDN'T KNOW I WOULD BE THIS EXCITED!" I said. "IT'S HARD TO CONTROL MY THRILL!"

After that, I looked at the beautiful fishes some more.

I smiled and smiled inside my head.

It was just like being in a *fish zoo*!

Only just then, a little bit of trouble happened.

And it's called, I spotted a stick behind a rock.

And then GULP!

The stick started to *move*!

And GASP!

OH NO, OH NO!

THE STICK SWAM AWAY!

'Cause it wasn't even a *STICK*, that's why!

It was . . .

"AN EEL! AN EEL! I SPOTTED AN EEL!" I screamed. "911! 911!! EEL SPOT-TING! EEL SPOTTING! HELP! HELP! HELP!"

Some of the other snorkelers popped up their heads.

Then Daddy popped up his head, too.

"*Shh*, Junie B.! *Shh!* There's nothing to worry about. I *promise*," he said. "That eel is perfectly harmless."

I quick ducked down again.

'Cause I had to keep track of the eel, of course!

Then WHOA! WAIT! HOLD THE PHONE!

Something even *worse* was floating my way!

And it's called . . .

"JELLYFISH! A JELLYFISH IS COMING!

AND THAT THING IS AS BIG AS A BARN,
I TELL YOU!"

After that, I quick turned around!

And I kicked for the beach as hard as I
could! And I didn't stop till I got there.

Then I ran out of the water.

And I tripped on my frog feet.

And I fell over in the sand.

I rested there to take a breather.

"Breathe," I said to my poundy heart.
"Breathe, breathe, breathe."

Just then, I heard sloshing feet.

I opened one eye.

It was Daddy.

His face did not look pleasant.

I waved my fingers very nervous.

"Hello. How are you today?" I said. "I am fine. Only I turned out to be afraid of jellyfish, apparently. So I swam to the beach. And then I tripped on my frog feet. And now I am resting comfortably in the sand."

I thought for a second.

"Also, I did not care for the eel."

Just then, Mother came hurrying out of the water.

She looked as grouchy as Daddy.

I waved again.

"Good to see you both," I said.

Daddy did a mad frown.

"This *isn't* a joking matter, young lady. You were supposed to stay with Mother and me," he said. "Don't you *ever* pull a stunt like that again. Do you understand?"

All of a sudden, my eyes got tears in them.

"But . . . but I didn't even mean to *pull* a stunt, Daddy. I just got scared. And I started to kick. And I didn't even know I would do that."

My nose started to sniffle very much.

"Sorry, Daddy. Sorry, Mother. Sorry I got scared."

Mother and Daddy looked at each other.

They didn't seem as mad anymore.

Mother sat down next to me.

"We're not mad at you for being *scared*, honey," she said. "We're upset because you swam away from us. You should never, *ever* swim alone in the ocean."

I sighed very glum.

"I turned out to be a chicken," I said.

"I am a chicken of the ocean."

Mother smiled and ruffled my hair.

"I think you mean chicken of the *sea*," she teased.

Then she and Daddy did a chuckle.

Only I don't actually know why.

After that, we walked back to the car.

My camera was in the backseat.

"Phooey. I still have to take a dumb snorkel picture for my assignment," I said. "I thought today's picture would be cute. But these photos just keep getting stupider and stupider."

I handed Mother the camera.

Then both of us walked back to the sand to take another dumb picture.

She blew a little bit of air in Squeezer to make him look more lively.

Then I posed as good as I could.
And *click-click*.

Day Three: HAWAII IS MAKING
A FOOL OUT OF ME.

7

Flower Head

                                  Day Four

Dear first-grade journal,

    I am writing this page on a stupid dumb tour bus.

    Stupid dumb tour bus is the grown-up word for there is nothing but old people on this thing.

    We are going on a nature hike.

A nature hike is when you look at plants and birds and ~~seenery.~~ scenery.

I cannot think of a worse activity.

Mother said I will get some good pictures today.

Big whoop.

      From,

      Junie B., I Do Not Want to Be Here

I closed my journal. And I did a huff.

"This stupid dumb bus trip is taking *forever*," I grumped.

Mother and Daddy rolled their eyes.

'Cause we hadn't actually left the parking lot yet.

I kept on grumping.

Then finally, finally, *finally* . . . the bus door closed. And we started to go.

A man in the front seat picked up a microphone.

"ALOOOOHAAAA!" he hollered.

All of the bus people sat there real silent.

Then a few of them said aloha back at him . . . only way quieter.

The man laughed. "Oh, come *on*. You can do better than that!"

"*ALOOOOHAAAA!*" he hollered again.

And so this time more people said it. But they still weren't loud enough for him, I guess. Because we went through that same nonsense five more times.

I tapped on Mother. "This guy is getting on my nerves," I said.

"Shh," she said back.

I looked at Squeezer. "Being shushed is getting on my nerves, too," I said.

The man kept talking.

He said his name is Donald. And he will be our nature guide today.

I did a sigh.

"Little children do not like nature," I said.

Donald kept on blabbing. He said we were on our way to a beautiful rain forest. And we will see some of the most spectacular scenery in the world.

I covered my face.

"Little children *hate* spectacular scenery," I said.

Donald went on. He said we will see gorgeous flowers and magnificent trees and beautiful birds of all colors.

I did a loud groan.

"Can this situation get any *boringer*?" I said.

An old man in front of me heard me say that.

He peeked his head over the seat real friendly.

He said his name was Harold. And he was "eighty-eight years young."

"When you get to be my age, spectacular scenery is as exciting as it gets," he said.

I sighed again. "That's not much to look forward to, Harold," I said.

Daddy quick leaned over. And he told me to *please find something to do*.

Then he gave me my camera. And he said to take a picture of the people on the bus.

I waited till we stopped at a light. Then I stood in the aisle. And I took a picture.

Click-click.

Day Four: A BUS FULL OF OLD PEOPLE.

I sat back down.

"That picture will go nicely with my other embarrassing photo-journal pictures," I said. "Room One is going to laugh me right out of Show-and-Tell."

After that, Mother snatched my camera away. And she said maybe I needed a nap.

I covered my ears.

"Yeah, only how can I even sleep with all of Donald's yakking going on?" I said.

That man would not stop, I tell you.

He told us the names of a million jillion Hawaii birds and a million jillion Hawaii flowers. Plus also, he talked about pineapples, and coconuts, and bananas, and papayas.

Then Donald took a big breath. And he started talking about tuna fish!

I threw my hands in the air.

"FOR THE LOVE OF PETE! SOMEONE TAKE HIS MICROPHONE AWAY!" I hollered.

Mother did a gasp at that comment.

Daddy did a gasp, too.

I quick covered my mouth. But it was too late. All the bus people were stretching their necks to look at me.

"Junie B.! What on earth has gotten into you today?" asked Mother.

I slumped way down.

"Sorry, Mother. Sorry. But I've got stress in my head. 'Cause I *really* need an exciting picture for my photo journal. Only what kind of exciting picture can you get on a stupid dumb nature walk with old people?"

I stopped and looked over the seat.

"No offense, Harold," I said.

"None taken," he said back.

"It's just that I'm running out of time," I explained.

"Aren't we all," said Harold.

Mother sat me down again.

"Well, I can promise you one thing,

Junie B.," she said. "If you go on this hike with a bad attitude, *nothing* good will happen. But if you keep an open mind, you might be surprised. Sometimes nature can be very exciting."

I slumped down even more.

"Yeah, right . . . *exciting*," I said.

I turned and looked out the window.

I don't care what she says.

Nature is *not* exciting.

Not even if it's in paradise.

The bus trip took *forever,* it seemed.

But finally! Whew! At last! The driver turned a corner. And we pulled into a parking lot.

"We're here!" said Donald. "Welcome to our beautiful Hawaiian rain forest!"

I sprang up like a spring.

Then I ran outside. And I sniffed real deep.

"Fresh air! Fresh air! I thought I would never breathe you again!" I said.

Pretty soon, Donald gathered all of the bus people around him.

He gave us a nature-guide book. And he told us the hiking rules.

"*Hiking rule number one*," he said. "Please stay on the hiking trail and do *not* wander off on your own."

He went on. "*Hiking rule number two:* Please do *not* disturb the natural vegetation.

"And *hiking rule number three:* Please be respectful of nature and speak in quiet voices."

I looked at Squeezer and rolled my eyes.

"Wonderful. Another *quiet-voice* day," I grouched.

After that, all of the bus people lined up behind Donald. And we started hiking down the trail.

It was slow as molasses, I tell you. On account of every two seconds people kept stopping to look at stuff.

Just plain old normal *stuff,* I mean! Like plants and flowers and trees!

Finally, I got frustration in me.

"Okay, folks . . . keep it movin'. We've seen it all before," I called.

Daddy quick scooped me up. And he sat me on a rock.

Then he waited for the other bus people to pass by.

And big surprise.

I got scolded again.

He said if I can't behave myself, we will go back to the bus right now. And we will sit there until all the people come back.

"Is that what you want to do, missy?" he said. "Huh? Is it?"

I made a grump face.

"No, Daddy," I said. "I don't want to do *any* of this stuff. I wish we could do something exciting. 'Cause I've already *seen* flowers and nature before."

Just then, Mother picked up a flower that was lying on the trail.

"Oh, but you've never seen a flower quite like *this*, Junie B.," she said. "Look how beautiful this is. It looks like a big red powder puff!"

She stuck it in my hair.

Then she took out a mirror to let me see.

I stared at myself very admiring.

"Whoa," I said. "I look stunning."

Mother laughed. "Yes, you do," she said.

"This would make a really cute picture."

My face got brighter. "Hey, *yeah*!" I said. "This could be the first cute picture of my whole entire photo journal!"

I quick got my camera. And I held it way out in front of me.

Then *click-click*.

I took a picture of my very own self!

"Now *that* one is a keeper," I said.

I AM STUNNING!

After that, all of us started hiking again.

Only this time *I* was the slowpoke. 'Cause I kept picking up powder-puff flowers and sticking them in my hair.

Pretty soon, my whole head was full of those beautiful things.

I stuck extra ones in my pockets, and my shirt buttons, and my shoelace holes.

Then I looked down at Squeezer and smiled.

"Nature is being a little bit fun," I said.

I smiled bigger.

Who knew?

8

Clicking

We hiked and hiked to the end of the trail.

Then Donald gave us granola bars. Plus also, we drank Gatorade.

Donald liked my flower head.

"You look like a walking lehua blossom," he said.

I did a frown at that word.

"A le-who-a what-a?" I said.

"A *lehua blossom*. The flowers in your hair are red lehua blossoms," he explained. "Lehua blossoms are a favorite food source for a little red bird called an apapane."

I stared at that man for a real long time.

"You have way too much information in your head, Don," I said.

Donald laughed real loud.

Then I laughed, too.

Only it wasn't actually a joke.

After we rested, we started hiking back to the bus.

Mother and Daddy and I went last again. Only this time I had to walk even slower. On account of the flowers kept falling out of my hair. And so I had to keep picking them up and putting them back.

"Come *on*, Junie B.," said Mother. "We need to stay up with the others. If the flowers fall out of your hair, you'll just have to leave them."

I did a frown.

"But I worked very hard at this flower

arrangement," I said. "And I don't want to go back to the bus empty-headed."

Mother thought for a minute.

Then she picked up more flowers from the trail. And she wove them in all over my head. Plus also, she used some bobby pins to hold them.

"*There*. That ought to do the trick," she said. "Now come on. Let's go. We've *got* to catch up."

And so both of us started to run.

Only too bad for me.

Because all of a sudden, my shoe came loose. And so I quick sat down on the trail to tie it.

And that is the last pleasant hiking memory I have.

WHOOSH!

The noise zoomed by my ear.

WHOOSH!

I did a gasp!

A teensy red bird flew right by my face!

I sat there real frozen.

The bird fluttered and flapped. And chirped and twirped. And dipped and swirled.

And then—

PLOP!

THAT CRAZY BIRD LANDED RIGHT ON TOP OF MY HEAD!

My mouth tried to shout! But no words would come out.

I quick stood up and tried to shoo him away. But he just flapped and flopped and fluttered some more! And he kept right on staying there!

Then finally, my voice came back to normal!

"BIRD! BIRD! 911! 911! BIRD! BIRD! BIRD!" I screeched.

Mother and Daddy came running back to me.

Their mouths fell all the way open!

Then they tried to shoo the bird away, too. But it still kept flapping and flopping and fluttering up there!

Suddenly, Mother covered her mouth with her hand.

"Oh my gosh! I think it's stuck!" she said. "I think it's tangled in her hair!"

My eyes got big and wide at that news.

"*TANGLED?*" I yelled. "THE BIRD IS *TANGLED* IN MY HAIR? ARE YOU *KIDDING* ME?"

I raised my screech even louder.

"IT'S TANGLED! IT'S TANGLED! 911! 911! TANGLED BIRD!" I hollered.

All of the bus people came rushing back at once.

Plus Donald came rushing back, too.

He came to a stop in front of the group.

Then he quick gathered himself together. And he started giving orders.

"Okay. I need everyone to go back to the bus. *Now*," he said. "Please."

The old people hurried away.

Then Donald turned to Mother and Daddy. And he made his voice very calmy.

"Okay, Mom and Dad . . . step away from the bird," he said.

Mother and Daddy looked at each other. Then both of them stepped away.

After that, Donald walked to me real slow. And he squatted down next to me. And he held my hand.

"You okay, honey?" he said.

I rolled my eyes.

"I've got a bird on my head here, Don. How good can I be?" I said.

Donald smiled.

"I don't know. You look pretty brave to me," he said.

I thought for a minute and did a sigh.

"I'm not, Donald. I'm not brave," I said. "I'm afraid of jellyfish and eels."

Donald shrugged. "Join the club," he said.

After that, he gave me a pat. And he told me my final 'structions.

"Just hold your head perfectly still," he said. "I'm going to walk behind you and untangle this little guy, okay?"

My heart pounded real hard.

"Okay," I said back.

I stood as still as could be.

Donald's voice kept talking real quiet and calm.

"In all of my years as a nature guide, I have *never* seen a sight like this," he said.

I raised my eyebrows.

"Really, Donald?" I said.

"*Really,*" he said. "I wish I had a picture of this. A picture of this would be one in a million."

That's when it hit me!

I did a gasp.

"Donald . . . I have a *camera,*" I said.

I pointed to my backpack lying on the trail. "It's right in *there.*"

Mother covered her mouth.

"Oh my gosh. I completely forgot about that," she said.

Then she bent down real slow. And she got the camera from my backpack. And—

A BIRD IN THE HAIR!

Click-click.

She took a picture!

I kept on staying still.

I felt Donald pick up the bird real gentle.

And he untangled its feet from my hair.

Click-click.

Mother took another picture.

Then hurray!

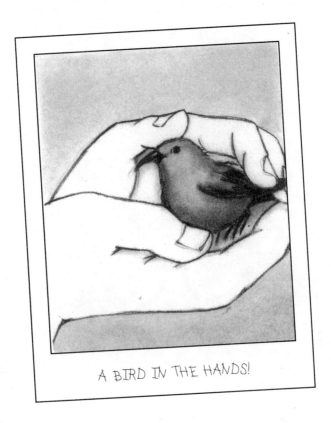

A BIRD IN THE HANDS!

Donald held out his hands. And he showed me the teensy little red bird.

"Look, see? Not one feather harmed," he said. "Good job, young lady."

I smiled real relieved.

"Good job to you, too, Donald," I said.

He winked at me.

"How about if you and I go release this little fella back to his tree?" he said. "He's going to have a pretty exciting story to tell all his friends, isn't he?"

I thought about Show-and-Tell. "Yes!" I said. "We *both* are!"

After that, I took the camera from Mother. And me and Donald went down the trail a little way.

Donald set the little bird on a rock.

He kept his hands around the bird real gentle.

"Ready?" said Donald.

"Ready," I said.

Donald took his hands away.

And *FLAP-FLAP!*

The bird started to fly.

I began snapping pictures very fast.

Click-click.

A BIRD IN THE TREE!

Click-click.

BYE-BYE, BIRDIE!

Then ZOOM! It flew away.
For a second, I stood there real silent.
Donald stood real silent, too.
"Whoa," I said finally.
"Wow," said Donald.
We looked at each other and smiled.
I aimed my camera one more time.
Click-click.

MY NEW FRIEND DON.

9

Aloha!

Day Five

Dear first-grade journal,

It is already tomorrow morning.

Mother and Daddy are still sleeping. Only I don't even know how they could even go to sleep at all last night!

'Cause yesterday was the excitingest day of my life!

Donald talked in the
microphone
~~microfone~~ the whole way
home.

He said that the bird was
just a baby. And it thought my
head was a giant flower,
probably.

Also he said how brave I was.
And that I was a ~~deliteful~~ delightful little
girl.

It was a very interesting
conversation.

But that was not even the
end of my exciting bird day!

On account of last night I
took a bubble bath. And

113

Squeezer got all warmish and soapish.

And what do you know?

He slipped right off with the bubbles!

I am getting to be excellent with birds!

Someday I will be a nature guy, probably.

I thought for a second.

Hmm. Or maybe I will be a photo-journal guy, possibly.

I tapped on my chin.

No, wait! Maybe I might like
to ~~arange~~ arrange hair flowers! 'Cause I
have a talent for that, too, I
believe.

> From,
> Junie B., Nature Guy
> and Other Possible
> Stuff

I put my pencil down and took out my
photo journal.

'Cause after the bus trip yesterday, we
went right to the drugstore. And we got my
pictures developed. And they turned out
beautifully, I tell you!

I showed them to Philip Johnny Bob and
Squeezer. They loved them very much.

Also, I tried to show them to Delores. But she was busy getting a facial.

After I finished looking at the pictures, I lined them up in my journal.

And I printed their captions all nice and neat.

I smiled as I read them.

Day One: GROUCHY LADIES.

Day Two: DOOFUS GIRL AND SQUEEZER.

Day Three: HAWAII IS MAKING A FOOL OUT OF ME.

Day Four: A BUS FULL OF OLD PEOPLE.

I AM STUNNING!

A BIRD IN THE HAIR!

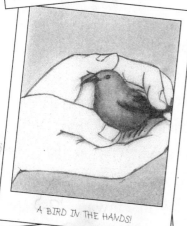

A BIRD IN THE HANDS!

A BIRD IN THE TREE!

BYE-BYE, BIRDIE!

MY NEW FRIEND DON.

Mr. Scary was right. A photo journal really *does* tell a story in pictures.

And Don was right, too! My bird picture was one in a million!

I did a sigh. "One in a million," I whispered. "You really can't beat one in a million."

I opened up my suitcase. And I packed my journal real careful.

I smiled some more. "Room One's first *official* photo journal ever," I said.

I stood up a little straighter.

'Cause feeling official made me taller again!

Just then, the radio went off. Today was going to be our last day in Hawaii. And so Mother and Daddy had set the alarm.

I looked at the clock and grinned.

There was still time for one more delicious pancake breakfast!

I tippytoed over to Daddy and blew air in his face.

He opened one eyeball.

I waved.

"Aloha-ha-ha," I whispered.

Daddy did a chuckle.

I kissed him on his cheek.

Hawaii was the time of my life.

People! People!
Read this next book
about my fun
in first grade!

Junie B., First Grader:
Dumb Bunny!

**Coming in
January 2007**

Don't miss these other funny books
by Barbara Park!

Rah! Rah! Rah!
Join the crowd.
Read these books
And laugh out loud!

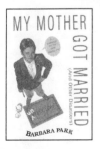   

BARBARA PARK is one of today's funniest authors. Her Junie B. Jones books are consistently on the *New York Times* and *USA Today* bestseller lists. Her middle-grade novels, which include *Skinnybones, The Kid in the Red Jacket, Mick Harte Was Here,* and *The Graduation of Jake Moon,* have won over forty children's book awards. Barbara holds a B.S. in education. She has two grown sons, one small grandson, and a medium-sized dog. She lives with her husband, Richard, in Arizona.

DENISE BRUNKUS'S entertaining illustrations have appeared in over fifty books. She lives in Massachusetts with her husband and daughter.